For Tess and Eli — RN
For my mom, who is afraid of ghosts — BE

Tundra Books, an imprint of Penguin Random House Canada Young Readers,
a Penguin Random House Company

Library and Archives Canada Cataloguing in Publication

Title: The little ghost who was a quilt / Riel Nason ;
illustrated by Byron Eggenschwiler.
Names: Nason, Riel, 1969- author. | Eggenschwiler, Byron, illustrator.
Identifiers: Canadiana (print) 20190207884 | Canadiana (ebook) 20190207892 |
ISBN 9780735264472 (hardcover) | ISBN 9780735264489 (EPUB)
Classification: LCC PS8627.A7775 L58 2020 | DDC jC813/.6—dc23

Published simultaneously in the United States of America by Tundra Books
of Northern New York, an imprint of Penguin Random House Canada Young
Readers, a Penguin Random House Company

Library of Congress Control Number: 2019952635

Edited by Samantha Swenson
Designed by John Martz
The artwork in this book was rendered with a combination of pencil drawings
and digital techniques.
The text was set in LTC Powell.

Printed and bound in China

www.penguinrandomhouse.ca

7   24   23   22

Penguin
Random House
TUNDRA BOOKS

THE
Little Ghost
WHO WAS A
Quilt

WRITTEN BY **Riel Nason**

ILLUSTRATED BY **Byron Eggenschwiler**

tundra

Once there was a little ghost
who was a quilt.

He didn't know why he was a quilt.
His mom and dad and all his
friends were sheets.

They were light as air. They flew high and fast and twirled and whirled in the sky.

They could even ride on a gust of wind and then WHOOSH back to the ground like they were going down an invisible slide.

The little ghost who was a quilt was heavy because of
his layers of fabric. It was hard for him to lift off,
and he was a slow flyer. He got hot and sweaty
when he tried to go faster. The only time
he attempted to twirl and whirl,
it didn't end well.

One day he and his friends were at the park when they heard someone coming. His friends zoomed away because ghosts are terrified of people. But the little ghost couldn't escape quickly enough.

He flopped over a bench. A family came along, and a little boy who was eating an ice cream cone sat down beside him. The little ghost had never been so close to a human before, and he felt fear in every fiber of his fabric. The boy only stayed a few minutes, but he dropped a big blob of melted ice cream right on the little ghost's face!

Later when some other ghosts saw him, they laughed at the stain on his forehead. The little ghost was embarrassed — and also very sticky.

The little ghost didn't like being different. His mom told him he had an ancestor who was a checkered tablecloth. And his great-grandmother was an elegant lace curtain. Everyone said she was the most beautiful ghost they'd ever seen. Even knowing that, the little ghost didn't feel any better.

He wished he was just one fabric and not a whole bunch of squares sewn together. The other ghosts called him Scrappy, and he didn't like that.

But there was one day that
always cheered him up:

Halloween!

People seemed excited about ghosts on Halloween, and sometimes children dressed as them to trick-or-treat.

Every year the ghosts went to watch the festivities. They stayed silent and still in the trees and pretended to be decorations, far away from any humans.

Too heavy to hover, the
little ghost who was a quilt
usually draped himself over
a clothesline. He never had a
very good view.

This year he had a better plan. He remembered how close he had been to the boy at the park, so he decided he would be brave and fold himself over a chair on a porch — right in the center of the action.

Halloween night came, and the little
ghost flew as fast as he could. But he
was only halfway across a lawn when
he heard people coming.

At the last possible second,
he flopped over the porch rail.

A mom walked up the driveway with a little girl dressed as a ballerina.

While the girl trick-or-treated, the mother asked the man at the door something.

The next thing the little ghost knew, the mom had picked him up! He was so scared he thought his seams might come unstitched.

The mom wrapped the little ghost
around the girl and put them both in
a wagon. The girl had been cold, and
now the little ghost was keeping her
warm. He could hardly believe what
was happening!

They headed down the street past his friends in their tree.
"Nooooo, dooooon't gooooo," one whispered.
"What are yooooouuu dooooooing?"

The little ghost decided to fly away as soon as the girl got out of the wagon to trick-or-treat again. But the mom didn't turn into the next yard. Or the one after that. By the time she finally walked up to a house, the little ghost was panicking. How would he get away?

The mother parked the wagon
and carried the girl and the little
ghost into the house. The little
ghost didn't know what to do!
He reminded himself to stay calm
and be brave.

The little ghost peeked around the room.
There were Halloween decorations everywhere.
He even saw a branch trimmed with lollipop ghosts!
They looked just like his friends in the tree.

The girl tucked the little ghost who was a quilt
under her legs as she sorted her candy into piles.
He felt surprisingly cozy. Maybe things would
turn out okay after all.

The girl ate a chocolate bar,
and when she wiped
her sticky fingers on
the little ghost, he
didn't even mind.

After the little girl was asleep
upstairs, her mom gently folded
the little ghost who was a quilt.
She smiled and admired his fabrics
and traced her finger along a line
of his stitching. It tickled.

She set the little ghost on the couch and went upstairs too. When she was gone, he flew into the fireplace and out the chimney.

His smile was
three squares wide.

The little ghost's friends cheered and rushed over to him. They were amazed by his courage and wanted to hear every detail of his adventure. They flew slowly along with him all the way home.

The little ghost was so happy that he felt like he was floating without even trying. Everything that had happened was because he was a little bit different. Everything had happened because he was a quilt.